Family

ISBN: 9781983165412

A Little Green Pea & WADDL Poetry Book

A Little Green Pea Publication, Reprinted 2020

Photography, content and design by Anna Carey.

Other publications and more information available at www.littlegreenpea.co.uk

little green pea

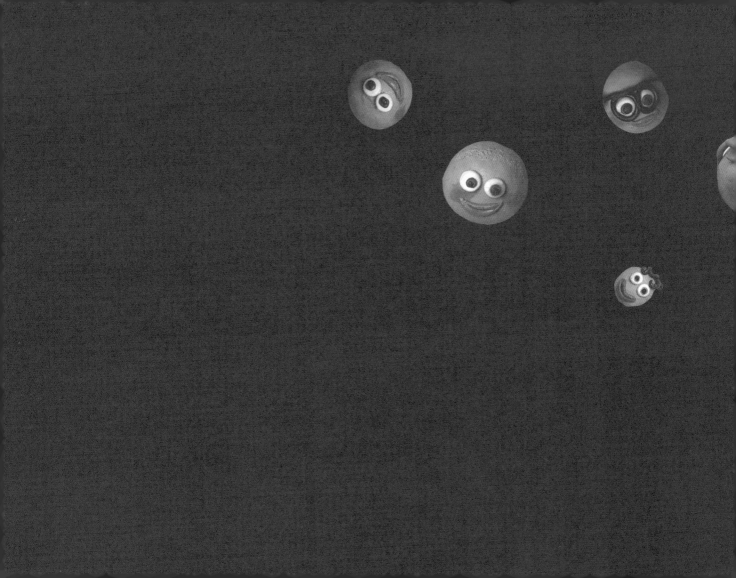

Have you met this family?
Please can they talk to you?

They want to tell you how they feel
and what they think and do...

Mimi Pea

I'm Mimi, always listening
and ready for a chat

but I can still get tired out
(do please remember that).

I love to hear your stories
but not to hear you fight,

my favourite things are "I love yous"
and kissing you goodnight.

Poppa Pea

I'm sometimes 'Grand-Pea', sometimes 'Dad'
but you can call me 'Pops'

they say I'm wise and thoughtful
because I've seen a lot.

You'll hear me say "I've seen it all"
but that is not quite true;

I love it when you talk to me
and teach me something new!

Super Pea

Today I'll be 'Sir Super Green'
not Bird, not Plane, but Pea!

I will never need a hero
if the rescuer is me!

So if you need some super powers
I'll show you I'm courageous

and if its cheering-up you need
my giggles are contagious.

unless...

you find me looking scared
or heading for a squish,

in which case you may save me
if you really do insist!

There are some things I do not like
for starters there is soup

and I get scared when frozen peas
don't let me in their group.

When I share these scary things
my fears all go away

but when I share my Super Powers
my smile stays all day!

Sweet Pea

I like being me, a sweet little pea
and I'm happy being green.

Just sometimes when I'm feeling sad
I'm accidentally mean

If I could change just one small thing
do you know what it would be?

I'd ask you all to take a turn
at being a tiny pea.

Hap-pea

When I was just a teeny pea
I had to leave my pod...

and move to a new family
at first it felt quite odd.

My brother and my sister pea
are cosy with me here

for now, at least, I do feel safe
as long as they are near.

So could I stay and snuggle-in,
away from trouble please?

Until the day I'm fully grown,
a bright green grown-up pea.

Then I'll say "I'm glad I moved"
and that, with you, I grew

and even if I've left this Pod
I'll always cuddle you.

The End

littlegreenpea.co.uk

How to use this book

This book (and others in the Little Green Pea collection) provide an engaging conversation starter about families and empathy,

A Personalised read:
The poems can be read at several different levels. On the surface they are just short poems from each pea character but in fact the characters have different experiences depending on their position in the pod. In this way, children can make comparisons with their own situation and be encouraged to share how they and other family members might feel about their 'pod'.

Building empathy for others:
By noticing differences in accounts of life in the pod and considering how peas can feel differently about being in the same pod, children are encouraged to consider whether these differences matter to them and what it might be like for each member of a real–life family sharing a home or living apart.

Schools Use:

Children can be asked to consider all the questions in the printable worksheets as well as using the book to facilitate discussion in the following curriculum areas;

- **Healthy Relationships**
- **Diversity**
- **Ethnicity**
- **Types of Family**
- **Myself , Self-identity**
- **Growth and Growing up**
- **Emotional Intelligence and Empathy**

Therapeutic Use:

On the website (below) you will find a FREE Download of worksheets to use with children. Specifically designed for use with parents or professionals, the guide and accompanying worksheets explore empathy, emotional intelligence and lead children toward identifying their trusted support network and 'safe peas' to share worries with.

If you found this guide helpful, visit www.littlegreenpea.co.uk for the FREE pack to accompany this book.

Printed in Great Britain
by Amazon